ZAMM
Is a Wonder

WITHDRAWN

Read more about Aleca's
adventures in book 2:

Aleca Zamm Is Ahead of Her Time

ALECA✲ZAMM
Is a Wonder

GINGER RUE

Aladdin
NEW YORK LONDON TORONTO SYDNEY NEW DELHI

This book is a work of fiction. Any references to historical events, real people, or real places are used fictitiously. Other names, characters, places, and events are products of the author's imagination, and any resemblance to actual events or places or persons, living or dead, is entirely coincidental.

ALADDIN

An imprint of Simon & Schuster Children's Publishing Division

1230 Avenue of the Americas, New York, New York 10020

First Aladdin paperback edition June 2017

Text copyright © 2017 by Ginger Stewart

Cover illustration copyright © 2017 by Zoe Persico

Also available in an Aladdin hardcover edition.

All rights reserved, including the right of reproduction in whole or in part in any form.

ALADDIN and related logo are registered trademarks of Simon & Schuster, Inc.

For information about special discounts for bulk purchases, please contact Simon & Schuster Special Sales at 1-866-506-1949 or business@simonandschuster.com.

The Simon & Schuster Speakers Bureau can bring authors to your live event. For more information or to book an event contact the Simon & Schuster Speakers Bureau at 1-866-248-3049 or visit our website at www.simonspeakers.com.

Cover designed by Karin Paprocki

Interior designed by Hilary Zarycky

The text of this book was set in ITC New Baskerville.

Manufactured in the United States of America 0517 OFF

2 4 6 8 10 9 7 5 3 1

Library of Congress Cataloging-in-Publication Data

Names: Rue, Ginger, author.

Title: Aleca Zamm is a wonder / by Ginger Rue.

Description: First Aladdin paperback edition. | New York : Aladdin, 2017. | Series: Aleca Zamm ; 1 | Summary: Aleca Zamm is ordinary compared with her sister and friends until her tenth birthday, when she discovers she can stop time just by saying her name, which could cure her test anxiety.

Identifiers: LCCN 2016032078 | ISBN 9781481470605 (pbk) | ISBN 9781481470612 (hc) | ISBN 9781481470629 (eBook)

Subjects: | CYAC: Ability—Fiction. | Magic—Fiction. | Friendship—Fiction. | Test anxiety—Fiction. | Schools—Fiction. | Humorous stories. | BISAC: JUVENILE FICTION / Fantasy & Magic. | JUVENILE FICTION / Social Issues / Friendship. | JUVENILE FICTION / Humorous Stories.

Classification: LCC PZ7.R88512 Ale 2017 | DDC [Fic]–dc23

LC record available at https://lccn.loc.gov/2016032078

For Martin H. Chambers,
because Aleca was born in your elementary school class.
I wish all children had a teacher like you
to believe in them.

CONTENTS

1

Everybody's Got a Thing but Me / 1

2

A Thing Called Mojo / 7

3

Time Stands Still / 13

4

I Blame the Posters / 25

5

Seizing a Hamster (and Opportunities) / 30

6

Nervous? Who's Nervous? / 38

7

Dance Like No One Is Watching (Because They're Not) / 42

8

Even More Secret Than Raspberry Filling / 49

9

This Time-Stopping Business Has Its Perks / 51

10

There's a Sherbet-Haired Lady in Our Car / 55

11

Aunt Zephyr Doesn't Fool Around / 61

12

My Grandfather, a Horse, and a Snake / 68

13

Zander Zamm Makes a Deal / 74

14

Wondering / 80

15

Aunt Zephyr Wanders and Wonders / 83

16

I'd Rather Be a Pretty Witch / 89

17

I'm Not a Dud . . . I'm a Wonder! / 94

18

There's a Downside to Everything / 99

19

Wondering Is Top Secret / 109

20

The One Time in History When Jolly Ranchers Didn't
Bring Happiness / 113

21

Something in the Lunchroom Is More Mysterious
Than the Food / 117

ALECA✳ZAMM
Is a Wonder

✳ 1 ✳

Everybody's Got a Thing but Me

"Maybe timed tests aren't your thing," my mom said as we waited in the car pool line before school.

"What *is* my thing?" I asked. "See, Mom? That's the thing. . . . I don't have a *thing*."

"Sure you do," Mom replied. "Everyone has a thing."

"Then what's mine?"

"Oh, Aleca, you're good at lots of things."

"Name one."

"Well," Mom began. "You're very good at . . . You're very . . . Well, you have a wonderful sense of humor."

"No I don't," I said. "I'm not good at telling jokes."

"But you laugh at all the right places in funny movies," Mom insisted.

"Laughing at stuff that's funny isn't a thing, Mom," I replied.

"Being a loser—that's your thing," said my sister, Dylan, from the front seat. She could be really mean sometimes, especially since she'd started middle school last year.

"Dylan, that was unkind and uncalled for," Mom scolded. "And on your sister's birthday, of all days." She made Dylan apologize and say happy birthday. Dylan did it, but she didn't mean it.

Deep down I knew Dylan was right. If I had a thing at all, it was being a loser.

It certainly wasn't singing, like Dylan . . . or swimming, like my best friend, Maria . . . or soccer or gymnastics or dancing or anything else.

And it sure wasn't math. Which was why I was so stressed out that morning.

It was Wednesday, so we were having another timed test. I'd practiced at home all weekend, but whenever Mrs. Floberg put a test on my desk, my hands got sweaty and the room started spinning. We were supposed to do fifty problems in three minutes, but I could never finish in time with a 90 percent or better. Which meant that I didn't get a Jolly Rancher when the tests were returned the following day. Pretty unfair, if you ask me, because (a) Jolly Ranchers are delicious, and (b) Jolly Ranchers given out by a teacher taste better. Don't ask me why; they just do. Plus, being forced to smell other people's blue raspberry and cherry Jolly Ranchers while you sit there math shamed is just plain WRONG.

"I know you're worried about the test today, Aleca," Mom said, "but all you can do is give it your best shot."

"It won't matter." I shook my head. "Mrs. Floberg hates me."

"I'm sure that's not true," said Mom. "Why wouldn't she like you?"

"Because Mrs. Floberg loves Madison, and Madison can't stand me."

"I can't imagine that your teacher would be childish enough to play favorites, Aleca."

"I don't have to imagine it. I live it. Mrs. Floberg knows how bad I am at math, but she always calls on me to work the hardest problems on the board," I insisted. "She does it to embarrass me."

"She's probably just trying to help you reach your full potential," Mom offered.

"Mrs. Floberg doesn't care about my potential," I replied. "Every time it's the same thing. She calls me up for the hardest problem, I stand there like a dork with no idea what the answer is, and then she says, 'Is there someone who has been paying attention, unlike Aleca?' And then Madison raises her hand and solves the problem, and Mrs. Floberg tells her how great and wonderful she is."

"I'm sure you're exaggerating, Aleca,"

Mom said. "Just try your best on the test. And think good thoughts about your birthday dinner tonight. I'm making all your favorites!" Mom stopped the car, and a safety patrol boy opened my car door. Mom called, "Good luck, sweetheart!"

The safety patrol boy snickered.

"Good luck, loser," Dylan called just as the safety patrol boy shut the car door.

I should've been mad at Dylan for calling me a loser again, but really . . . I figured I could use all the luck I could get.

✳ 2 ✳

A Thing Called Mojo

"Ten!" Maria squealed as she greeted me at the coat cubby. "Double digits! How does it feel?"

"You ought to know," I replied. Maria had turned ten two months before.

"I can't wait for your skating party!" Maria exclaimed. "And I can't wait to give you your present! You're going to love it!"

"Don't tell me what it is," I warned her. Maria had a hard time keeping secrets. Not that she was a blabbermouth or anything. She was just so honest (plus she got super-duper excited about giving presents).

"Of course I'm not going to tell you!" Maria said. "But do you want a hint?"

"Maria . . ." I was about to remind her that she always gave hints that were too big, but before I could, Madison and Jordan walked by. They were wearing white ribbons around their ponytails, the kind all the soccer girls wear.

"Our moms are making us come to your stupid party Saturday night," Madison said.

"Not that we want to," added Jordan.

"Wow, thanks," I said. Then I muttered, under my breath so they couldn't hear, "Don't do me any favors. Feel free to get sick or something."

Their ponytails bounced as they walked away.

Maria said something under her breath too, and at first I thought she said we ought to chase them, which didn't seem like the best idea. But what she actually said was, *"No manches,"* which is what Maria says when she means "unbelievable," because she knows two languages. Then she added, "In cartoons there are always anvils or pianos falling out of the sky and whacking bad people on the head. Why can't that happen in real life?"

Maria always knew how to make me feel better. In first and second grade Madison had been our friend. We had done everything together. Our parents had called us the Three Amigas. But then Madison joined cer team with Jordan. That was the end of the Three Amigas. I tried playing too, but I was klutzy. The other girls on the team were always mad at me for messing up. Mom let me quit even though she'd paid the fee for the full season. Maria hadn't tried to play soccer. She'd been too busy with swim team.

"Can't you just picture the two of them, squished from a falling anvil?" I said.

"With the big flat spot on their heads?" Maria added. "Or folded up and making that accordion sound when they walk?" We both giggled. Then Maria turned serious again. "So, are you ready for the test?"

"As ready as I'll ever be," I replied. "Ask me something."

Maria fired off a few division problems. I answered them all perfectly . . . and fast.

"This is it," Maria declared. "You're going to ace this one."

"I can always answer the questions . . . until the test comes," I fretted. "Then I freak out. Why should today be any different?"

"Because today you have mojo!" Maria said.

"What is mojo?" I asked. "Is it a disease?" I put my hand on my forehead. I didn't know why, exactly, but that's what my mom does whenever I get sick.

"Mojo is like . . . a good, special luck. A kind of magic."

"What makes you think I have any of *that*?" I asked.

"I don't know. I just have a feeling your luck is about to turn around. Today is the day everything changes for Aleca Zamm."

Today is the day everything changes for Aleca Zamm. I said Maria's words in my head over and over. I wanted to believe her. I wanted to have mojo, and lots of it. But I didn't hold out much hope.

It turned out that Maria was right.

❋ 3 ❋

Time Stands Still

When class began, however, I didn't feel any mojo at all. Nothing seemed to be changing for the better. In fact, everything seemed to be worse.

As soon as everyone was seated, Mrs. Floberg clapped her hands and announced, "Class, I have to step out of the room for a moment." I thought it was kind of illegal for a teacher to leave kids alone in the room without an adult, but if it was, Mrs. Floberg didn't seem to care. "While I'm gone, I expect you to be on your best behavior. No talking whatsoever."

Brett Lasseter high-fived one of his friends. There was some giggling from another area of the room.

"But just to be certain," continued Mrs. Floberg, "Madison, I'd like you to come up to the board and take names."

Madison walked up to the whiteboard and took the purple marker from Mrs. Floberg like she was accepting an award for discovering a new planet or something.

"Madison, if anyone so much as whispers, you write their name on the board. And put a check mark next to their name for every time they misbehave again. Understand?"

"Yes, Mrs. Floberg," Madison practically sang.

"I will be right back," Mrs. Floberg reminded us. Then she left the room.

No one uttered a word. Madison stood at the board eyeing all of us. She had this big I'm-the-boss-of-you grin on her face.

All of a sudden she turned to write a name on the board. I wondered who had spoken; I hadn't heard anything.

When she started writing a big purple *A*, I couldn't believe it. By the time she had finished the *l-e-c-a*, I was outraged.

"I didn't talk!" I protested.

Madison put a check mark next to my name.

"That's not fair!" I fumed.

Madison put a second check mark.

"You can't do that!" I said.

Another check mark.

"Who do you think Mrs. Floberg's going to believe? You or me?" Madison said with a mean grin.

She had a point.

But wait! I had a roomful of witnesses!

"Everyone in this room knows you're lying!" I pointed out.

Madison grinned even more wickedly. "Raise your hand if you will tell Mrs. Floberg that Aleca didn't talk."

Only one hand went up. Maria's.

So Madison wrote Maria's name on the board right under mine.

Maria made a face of terror. She'd never gotten in trouble in her life.

It was one thing for Madison to torment

me, but I couldn't let her do this to Maria.

"That's it!" I cried. I went up to the board and tried to wrestle the marker out of Madison's hand. I had almost gotten the purple symbol of injustice out of her grip, when I heard my name.

"Aleca!"

Mrs. Floberg was back. "What in the world do you think you're doing?"

Not only was Mrs. Floberg back, but she'd brought the principal, Mr. Vine, with her. Mr. Vine was skinny and tall and had a curved posture, all of which made him look kind of like, well . . . a vine. He had a face like a hound dog, all sad and droopy, and he always had two lines between his eyebrows, like maybe he had been thinking about something for a long time, and even though

17

his brain was finished thinking about it, his face wasn't yet.

"It's not what it looks like," I began. "It—"

"Mrs. Floberg!" Madison interrupted. "Thank goodness you're here! Aleca was talking and wouldn't stop, and when I put her name on the board and put the checks beside it, she went nuts and attacked me!"

"I did not!" I argued.

"That's exactly what happened," said Jordan. "Isn't it, everybody?"

I wouldn't say that everyone agreed, but some people said yes, and some didn't say anything. Only Maria spoke up to defend me.

"It's not true," Maria insisted.

"You can't believe her," Madison said. "She's Aleca's friend. And she was talking too. That's why her name is on the board."

"Maria, I'm surprised at you," Mrs. Floberg scolded. "It's not like you to be dishonest."

"I think Aleca's been a bad influence on her," Madison suggested.

"Are you kidding me?" I spluttered, and then turned to Mrs. Floberg. "You're not really going to believe any of this, are you?"

"Young lady, I know what I saw. Mr. Vine, this student has 'trouble' written all over her. I think it's time you take stern action to modify her behavior before it gets any worse."

"That sounds like a good idea," Mr. Vine replied with a frown.

"But I didn't do anything!" I realized I had just raised my voice at the principal, but I couldn't help it. It was all so unfair!

"How dare you raise your voice at me!" Mr. Vine exclaimed. He took a notebook and pen out of his suit pocket. "What is your full name?"

"Aleca Zamm," I said softly.

I braced myself for what would come next.

But Mr. Vine didn't say anything.

Neither did Mrs. Floberg.

Or anyone else.

In fact, the whole room became quiet. Scary quiet. I looked at Mr. Vine. He was as still as a statue. His eyebrows were knitted together in a scowl. I turned my head to look at Mrs. Floberg. She was also as still as a statue.

No one in the entire classroom was moving at all. Everything was silent.

"Mrs. Floberg," I said. "Are you all right?" No answer. "Mr. Vine?" No answer. "What's going on?" I demanded. "Is this some kind of joke?" Not a sound. Not a movement from anyone. "Maria? Maria, what's happening?" But not even Maria made a sound. She was completely still. Her shoulders were rounded and she had a worried look on her face. "Maria? Are you okay?" No answer.

Slowly I took a step away from the whiteboard and began to look around the room. Madison had gone over to Jordan's desk. Her hand was frozen, cupped to Jordan's ear. Brett and his friends, their teeth bared in evil smiles, looked almost like wolves. Everyone in the room was completely motionless. Joanie Buchanan was bent over a book. Neal Martinez was tying his shoe.

Scott Sharp was picking his nose. Ewww! I'd seen enough.

I went back to Mrs. Floberg and kind of shook her by the arm. Nothing. She was as stiff as a board. "What am I supposed to do here?" I said out loud. No response. Everything stayed exactly the same.

What *was* I supposed to do?

If Mom and Dad had gotten me a cell phone for my birthday, I could've called them. But no. *Fourth graders don't need cell phones,* they'd said. *That's just ridiculous.* Yeah, because it's not like a fourth grader would need to call home when everyone in her classroom turns to stone. *If you need to call us, you can use the office phone,* they'd insisted.

The office phone!

I eased past Mr. Vine and out the classroom door.

The entire school was quiet. I looked in classrooms along the way to the office, and they were just like mine—motionless. The door to the gym was open, and Coach Blanton was holding his hands out to catch a basketball he'd tossed up. The ball hung in the air above him like some ugly orange chandelier.

Mrs. Becky, the school phone answerer, was at her computer. Her fingers were curled above the keys. Only her right pinky finger touched a *p* on the keyboard.

I guessed she wouldn't mind if I used the phone without asking permission first.

I picked up the receiver. No dial tone.

"Come on," I pleaded. I hung up a few

times to see if it would click, but nothing happened. Just more silence.

The clock on Mrs. Becky's computer said 8:03 a.m.

I had no idea what to do. I sat down in one of the office chairs and waited for what felt like a long time.

But when I looked back at the clock on the computer, it still said 8:03 a.m.

✳ 4 ✳

I Blame the Posters

Maybe my school was caught in some sort of time warp.

I finally had the idea to look outside.

I could see cars stopped in the middle of the street across from the school building. The branches on the big tree behind the school marquee were bent to the left, like the wind that had blown them had never finished the job. A bug on the outside of the window wouldn't move even when I tapped the glass.

This was definitely weird.

I tried the phone again. Still no dial tone.

I walked back to Mrs. Floberg's room. Everything I passed was exactly as it had been before, right down to Coach Blanton's basketball floating above him.

I eased past Mr. Vine once again and walked over to Mrs. Floberg. "Mrs. Floberg, can you hear me?" I asked a few times, but she never responded. I even did a funny dance around the room, but nobody moved so much as a muscle.

I got right up in Mrs. Floberg's face and studied her. I could see goo in the inside corner of her left eye. I could see hair sprouting from the mole on her cheek. Her mouth was kind of open. I counted five fillings in her teeth.

"Won't somebody say something?" I yelled. "Anybody?"

Nothing.

"Okay, Aleca. Think," I said out loud. Sometimes when I get nervous, I do that—talk to myself. Dad once told me I shouldn't worry about being flaky unless I started answering myself too.

On TV detective shows when there's a mystery, the detective, who is smarter than everyone else, retraces her steps. I decided that would be the smart thing to do in this situation. "What just happened here?" I went through the whole thing word for word as well as I could remember.

"Then Mr. Vine asked who you are." It all

seemed simple enough. "You didn't do any-thing," I told myself. "All you said was 'Aleca Zamm.'"

Suddenly I heard noise again. The class-room had come back to life. Mrs. Floberg and Mr. Vine were no longer statues.

"What's that name again?" Mr. Vine said, putting his pen to his notepad.

"Aleca Zamm," I repeated.

Once again everything stopped.

"Seriously?" I said. I guess I was talking to myself again, since no one else was listening.

I sat down for a while to think.

Saying my name made time stop. Saying my name again made time start back up.

Saying my name!

What was up with *that*?

I looked around the room.

On the bulletin board next to the cluster of desks where Maria sat, Mrs. Floberg had hung a bunch of posters.

One was an eagle soaring in a blue sky. It said, "Change Your Thoughts, and You Change Your World."

Another one, with mountains, said, "Believe You Can, and You're Halfway There."

And one with no picture at all, just a multicolored background, said, "Seize Every Opportunity."

I thought about that last one for a while: Seize Every Opportunity.

"Okay, Mrs. Floberg," I said out loud. "I will."

❄ 5 ❄

Seizing a Hamster
(and Opportunities)

Remember that bug on the outside of the school office window? He didn't move at all when I picked him up.

Not even when I put him into Brett Lasseter's open mouth.

I took a bottle of glue out of Jordan's desk and squirted some over Madison's and Jordan's hair. "Now you two can *really* stick together," I said. I couldn't help but giggle. I really crack myself up sometimes.

Now. What to do with Mrs. Floberg and Mr. Vine?

Oh yes. Perfect.

I walked down the hallway to the first-grade classroom that was home to Wendell the Hamster. Wendell had been spinning merrily in his wheel when time had stopped. Now he was floating in the air, midrun.

I scooped him out of his cage and petted him for a while. You'd think it would be fun to pet a hamster for that long without it trying to escape, but it was really just like holding a stuffed animal, which is kind of fun but not the kind of fun that lasts very long before you get bored. I took Wendell back to my classroom. I placed him in the folds of Mrs. Floberg's scarf.

Then I inspected Mr. Vine. His jacket

had shifted when he'd gotten the pen and notepad out of his pocket to write down my name. I could see that he wore suspenders to hold up his pants.

That one was almost too easy.

But the poster did say *every* opportunity.

Was there anything else? Anything I was overlooking?

Oh yes. The math test was in a file on Mrs. Floberg's desk. Nobody would know if I sneaked a peek.

"Mrs. Floberg," I said, "would you mind if I took a look at the math test?"

She didn't say she'd mind.

"If you think it would be wrong for me to look at it, just say so," I stated.

She didn't say anything.

"If you are one hundred percent perfectly

okay with me looking at the test, just don't say anything," I went on.

She didn't say a word.

That was pretty much permission, wasn't it? And even if it wasn't exactly permission, well . . . I deserved a little extra help, didn't I? Maybe it wasn't really fair to see the test beforehand, but was it fair the way Mrs. Floberg humiliated me in front of the class all the time? Was it fair that she made me work the hardest problems on the board when she knew that I couldn't get the right answer? Was it fair that no matter how much I studied, I never even once got a Jolly Rancher, and the other kids who didn't have to study always got them and ate them right in front of me?

I decided that life is full of unfairness

and that, for once, that ought to work in my favor.

I took a few minutes (I guess it was minutes—the clock on the wall had stopped, so I couldn't say for sure) and went over the problems. I memorized the answers for the first couple of rows so that when I got the test, I wouldn't even have to stop and do the problems.

I went back to where I'd been before I'd stopped time. "Aleca Zamm!" I said.

Just like before, everything went back to normal.

Except that Mrs. Floberg screamed and swatted at her neck as Wendell jumped from her scarf to my desk cluster. (Joanie Buchanan caught him before he could run away.) Meanwhile, Madison and Jordan wailed about the glue in their hair, and Brett Lasseter began spitting and crying because of the bug that came to life in his mouth. And at the exact same time, Mr. Vine's suit pants fell to his ankles. The class laughed their heads off (except for Madison and Jordan, who were still wailing, and Brett, who was still spitting and crying). Also, I think it is worth mentioning here that Mr. Vine's boxer shorts had little sailboats all over them. No wonder everyone laughed so hard. Because for the rest of our lives, whenever we see a sailboat, we will all think of Mr. Vine's underwear, and there is nothing he can do to change that.

Eventually Mr. Vine got his pants back up and Mrs. Floberg stopped screaming. Joanie asked for permission to take Wendell back to the first-grade hall. Then Mrs. Floberg finally remembered that I was in big trouble.

"You!" she bellowed. "This is all your fault!"

"How could any of this be my fault?" I asked innocently.

"I'm sure this is all just a very strange mis-understanding," Mr. Vine said. He was hold-ing the waist of his pants up, just in case. "Now, if you'll excuse me . . ." He rushed out of the room, his face still red.

"You heard Mr. Vine," I said. "A strange misunderstanding."

Mrs. Floberg sighed. "Very well," she said. She leaned in and warned, "I can't prove any-thing this time. But I'm watching you." Then she announced to the whole class, "Please clear your desks. We have a test to take."

I couldn't wait to get started on the test. Because I knew that the Jolly Rancher I would get tomorrow when Mrs. Floberg gave back the tests would be the best candy of my whole entire life!

✳ 6 ✳

Nervous? Who's Nervous?

"I can't believe you finished the whole test in time!" Maria chattered at lunch. "And you really think you'll get a hundred?"

"I'm pretty sure I will."

"I am so happy for you!" Maria said.

"Thanks. Me too." And I guess I was. I mean, it all felt kind of strange.

"I just knew things were going to start going your way. Something just told me, today is Aleca's day! Things are supposed to go your way on your birthday, right?"

"Sure," I agreed. "By the way, did you have any other . . . I don't know . . . interesting feelings today?"

"Not really." Maria shook her head. "But wasn't it weird how Wendell got into our room? All the way from the first-grade hall?"

"Yeah. Weird."

"And how he just popped up in Mrs. Floberg's scarf, of all places?"

"Yeah, of all places."

"And at the exact same time that Mr. Vine's pants fell down!"

"Yeah, exact same time."

"I wonder how that glue got into Madison's and Jordan's hair—and that bug in Brett's mouth!"

"Yeah, I wonder."

"No manches," Maria said. "Aleca, do you know something you're not telling me?"

"No. Why would you think that?"

"Well, for one thing, you're not saying much. And for another thing, you just put mini chocolate chips in your hummus."

She was right. The mini chocolate chips were supposed to go in my vanilla yogurt. The carrot sticks were supposed to go in the hummus. "Haven't you ever had chocolate chips in your hummus?" I asked innocently.

"Um, no."

"You're missing out, then. It is what they call a taste sensation." I took a big scoop of the mixture with a carrot stick and put it into my mouth. It tasted just how you would expect chocolate chips and hummus to taste—awful. "Mmmm!" I said, trying not to barf. "Yum! Want some?"

"No, thanks," Maria replied. "But are you sure you're okay? You seem a little . . . shaken up."

"Shaken up? Me? Why would I be shaken up?"

Maria shrugged.

"If there is one thing I'm not, it's shaken up," I assured her.

Just because I'd stopped and started time—TWICE—cheated on a test, put a hamster in the teacher's clothing, and showed our principal's underwear to my entire class, that was no reason to be shaken up.

Neither was lying to your best friend—for the first time ever.

Okay, so maybe I was a little shaken up.

41

❋ 7 ❋

Dance Like No One Is Watching (Because They're Not)

For the rest of the school day, I was pretty quiet. Which was probably good, because Madison was really gunning for me. She couldn't explain the glue incident, but she sensed I'd had something to do with it. So I kept to myself. I didn't talk much, even to Maria. Paying attention in class was almost impossible. All I could think about was how I'd stopped time earlier that day.

I stopped time, I kept repeating in my head. *I actually stopped time.*

I'd never heard of anything like it. Could other people do it too? I doubted it. I was pretty sure I would have heard about that somewhere down the line.

But now what was I supposed to do? Should I tell my parents when I got home? I didn't think so. I just felt like probably I would get in trouble for time stopping. I didn't think that would be entirely fair, because no one had ever told me *not* to stop time. It's not like my parents ever said, *Aleca, stopping time is not allowed.* It wasn't the kind of thing that just comes up. *Aleca, don't stop time, don't paint polka dots on elephants, and don't fill the bathtub with Skittles.* (I'd always sort of wanted to do that last one.)

And of course, if I couldn't tell my parents, I couldn't tell Dylan. She'd tell on me faster than I could say "Aleca Zamm" to stop time to keep her from telling.

Then I thought maybe I could tell Maria. But that seemed risky too, since Maria can't even keep a birthday present secret. But maybe with something as important as this, she'd do a better job. But I figured that even if I did tell Maria, first I'd have to figure out what was going on so she wouldn't be too freaked out.

If I couldn't tell Maria or Dylan or my parents, who was I supposed to tell?

I was going to have to keep this to myself. Which was harder than you might think, because it was either the scariest or the coolest thing that had ever happened to me in my whole life.

I decided to figure out the answer to that question. Was being able to stop time scary, or cool? I considered it while I was supposed to be listening to Mrs. Floberg lecture about the Civil War.

On the one hand, stopping time was scary, because I'd never done it before that day. And because . . . Well, I couldn't really think of any other becauses.

On the other hand, stopping time was cool. Because probably it could come in handy in all sorts of situations, like sleeping late, or when you want to think of a good, snappy comeback and your mind goes blank. Because it gave me an advantage to be able to walk around and see things and do things when no one else knew what I was seeing and doing. Because I could do all this and then just as easily start time up again when I was good and ready.

So the more I thought about it, the less scared I felt and the more excited I became.

Just for fun I decided to stop time again, so while Mrs. Floberg was saying something about 1861, I whispered, so that no one else could hear, "Aleca Zamm."

And everything stopped, just like it had before.

Nothing was all that different from how it had been the first time. Joanie still had her nose in a book. Madison and Jordan were leaning in to each other, whispering. Brett had one raised eyebrow and flared nostrils. I think this is because sometimes he needs extra oxygen so he can be extra mean. And as for Scott Sharp . . . wow, did that guy ever do anything besides pick his nose? You'd think he'd eventually run out of boogers.

I went over to Maria's desk. She was taking notes, which didn't surprise me. She makes straight As. I took her pencil out of her hand for a minute and drew a smiley face in the corner of her paper. When I started time again, maybe she would see it and not remember drawing it but feel happy that it was there.

After that I couldn't really think of anything else I wanted to do, so I did a weird little tap dance—I don't actually know how to tap, so that's why it was weird—and sat back down. I decided that whenever I stopped time, I should do a dance to put a kind of "ta-da" on it, because one time Dylan had this T-shirt that said, "Dance Like No One Is Watching." But how many people get to actually do that in a room full of people? Probably nobody but me, so it seemed like it was my duty. I made a mental note to look up videos of dances so that maybe I could do a different one each time.

I said my name again, and Mrs. Floberg just kept right on about whatever it was that happened in 1861. (I still wasn't listening.)

I had decided. Stopping time—definitely cool.

✳ 8 ✳

Even More Secret Than Raspberry Filling

My birthday dinner that night was fun. Mom made my favorite—cheese-steak sandwiches. My cake was lemon raspberry. The lemon part is in the cake and in the icing, and the raspberry part is in between the two layers of cake. You don't even know it's there until the cake is cut. So it's almost like the cake has a secret. So me and the cake had something in common.

Because I most def had a secret, which

I kept. Even though Mom and Dad asked me how my day was. And even though Dylan was actually kind of nice to me and gave me a present—a leather bracelet like the ones that she and her cool middle school friends wore. Mom and Dad gave me a pair of pink sneakers and a gift card for some new apps for my iPad. Also, they were letting me have my party Saturday at Super Skate!

After two cheese-steak sandwiches and a big piece of cake, I watched my favorite TV show, took my bath, and went to bed.

My tenth birthday had been the best one so far.

✳ 9 ✳

This Time-Stopping Business Has Its Perks

"Aleca, wake up, honey," my mom said the next morning. Mom is always the one who wakes me up gently. She does that about three times before my dad finally has to say in his stern voice, "Aleca, feet on the floor!" That's when I actually get up.

But this time when Mom left my bedroom, I felt really tired. And I remembered what a good day I'd had yesterday, and then I got this great idea.

Why should I have to get up if I didn't want to?

"Aleca Zamm," I said. Everything in the house got quiet. I could have gotten up to check that everything had stopped, but I was too tired. Then I remembered about my dancing-when-no-one-was-watching deal. Problem was, I didn't want to get out of bed. So I did a very unjazzy jazz hands real quick, and then I rolled over and went back to sleep. I figured if time hadn't stopped, I would still have a couple of more gentle Mom wake-ups and one stern Dad wake-up to get me going.

But that didn't happen. Instead I just slept for a while (I'm not sure how long, since my clock stopped) and then woke up when I felt ready.

Downstairs Mom was standing over the

stove, scrambling an egg. Dad was in their bedroom, tying his necktie. Dylan was in her closet, picking an outfit for the day.

I went back up to my room, got dressed, and then came back downstairs. I felt very extra rested.

"Aleca Zamm," I said. The stove began sizzling, and Mom stirred the eggs.

"My, you got ready in a hurry this morning," she said.

As I started to put the chocolate syrup into my milk, I realized that I had been so happy about my birthday and my new stopping-time thing the day before, I hadn't done any of my homework.

"Aleca Zamm," I said.

I finished up my language arts worksheet and did my math page. I could've actually used some help with the math, but of course no one could help, so I just did my best.

I put my work into my backpack, said "Aleca Zamm" once again, and ate breakfast. Then we piled into the van like always and Mom drove Dylan and me to school just like any other day.

This new ability was very convenient.

❅ 10 ❅

There's a Sherbet-Haired Lady in Our Car

I stopped time at school only twice that day. Once because there was a pop quiz on the Civil War, and I needed to go back and check my answers since I hadn't listened to anything during the lecture the day before, and once to go swing on the playground for a few minutes because I was bored. It was okay, but it wasn't as fun without Maria.

Also not fun: Mrs. Floberg hadn't graded

our math test yet, so I wouldn't get my Jolly Rancher for a whole extra day.

As I waited for Mom in the car pool line that afternoon, I wasn't thinking about time stopping. All I was thinking about was getting another slice of my birthday cake when I got home. But as soon as I got into the car, I knew immediately that something was weird.

Dylan was in the back, where I always sat, instead of up front as usual.

In Dylan's seat up front was an old lady with orange hair. Not red. Orange, like she had dipped her head in melted orange sherbet. I wondered if she'd had an accident or if she *wanted* to look that way.

"Hi, Mom," I said when I got into the car.

"Hello, sweetie," she replied. "Aleca, I'd like you to meet Aunt Zephyr."

"Hello," I told the lady. "*Aunt* Zephyr?" My mom had a couple of sisters, so I had two aunts on her side of the family, but my dad was an only child. So who was this person?

"*Hallo, olá, alo,*" said Aunt Zephyr. "*Selamat tengah hari.*"

I looked at Dylan. "Does she speak English?"

"Don't be ridiculous. Of course I speak English," muttered Aunt Zephyr.

"Oh, sorry," I said.

"Aunt Zephyr is extremely well traveled," Mom explained. "She was saying hello like they do in other countries."

"Iceland, Portugal, Romania, and Malaysia, to be precise," Aunt Zephyr announced.

"Good to know." Dylan rolled her eyes.

"Neither irony nor sarcasm is argument," Aunt Zephyr said to Dylan.

"Huh?" Dylan asked.

"That's a quote from Samuel Butler," she replied. "He's my favorite Victorian-era satirist. Who's yours?"

Dylan looked at me as if to say, *What is up with the old lady?* I shrugged.

"So, how are we related, exactly?" I asked.

"Aunt Zephyr is your great-aunt," Mom told us. "She's your father's father's sister."

"I didn't know Dad had any aunts or uncles," Dylan said.

"Well, your father's family was spread out, you might say," clarified Mom. "Aunt Zephyr has lived all over the world."

All this was very interesting, I supposed, but I couldn't figure out why Dad had never mentioned an aunt or an uncle. He barely spoke of his own parents. They'd died before he and Mom had gotten married, so I'd never even met them. And why, if his aunt was never so much as mentioned in my whole life before now, was she suddenly riding in our car?

I tried to think of how to ask that question without sounding rude.

"What brings you to town, Aunt Zephyr?" I inquired. That sounded grown-up and not rude.

Aunt Zephyr turned around and looked me dead in the eye. "Oh, I bet you could guess what brought me to town if you think hard enough."

Aunt Zephyr turned back around. Dylan looked at me again with the there's-a-lunatic-in-our-car face.

"Aunt Zephyr flew in unexpectedly," Mom said brightly. "We'll talk about it more when your father gets home."

Mom sounded nervous. Which made me nervous. Which made me wonder, with all the weird things that had already happened to me over the past two days, could things possibly get any weirder?

✳ 11 ✳

Aunt Zephyr Doesn't
Fool Around

When we got home, Dad's car was already in the driveway. That was definitely unusual. Dad always got home a little after six, just in time for dinner.

He was standing at the front door, looking kind of sweaty. He wasn't breathing hard, so I figured he must be nervous-sweaty instead of running-laps-sweaty.

"Aunt Zephyr! Are you all right? Was the travel difficult on you?" He grabbed her suitcase, which was sitting by the door, and we followed him into the living room.

Aunt Zephyr patted Dad's cheek, then squeezed it as though he were a little boy. "Skippy, you haven't changed a bit."

Skippy? For the third time in less than an hour, Dylan and I exchanged looks.

"I'm lying, of course," Aunt Zephyr continued. "Your temples are graying, you've put on a few pounds, and you're developing jowls. But of course these things can't be helped. Age is a cruel fact of life."

Dad laughed nervously. "Well, you certainly haven't lost your . . . candor."

"That's the trade-off for getting old," she replied. "The older you get, the more candid you can become. Old folks are allowed a certain degree of eccentricity."

"What does that mean?" I wondered.

"It means that the older you get, the more likely people are to put up with your weirdness," Aunt Zephyr replied.

"I am never going to be weird," Dylan announced.

"You're so right, my dear," Aunt Zephyr agreed. "My condolences."

Dylan turned to Mom. "What is that supposed to even mean?"

Mom patted Dylan and told her to go start her homework. Dylan stormed out of the room.

"Good," Aunt Zephyr said. "Now that the Dud is gone, we can get down to business." Then she looked at Mom and Dad. "No offense to you other Duds, of course."

"None taken," said Dad.

"What?" Mom asked. "'Duds'?"

"Please do not take the word pejoratively," Aunt Zephyr said. "I meant no offense. That's just the term we use."

Mom had always told me that one way to avoid an argument was to change the topic of conversation. I guessed that was why she said, "Not that we aren't thrilled to see you, Aunt Zephyr, but what brings you to town so suddenly? We haven't seen or heard a peep from you since Alec and I got married."

"Skippy, how much have you told the Mrs.?" Aunt Zephyr asked.

"A little," Dad answered. "Not much, really."

Aunt Zephyr raised an eyebrow, making her forehead wrinkles even deeper.

Dad cleared his throat. "Okay," he said.

"Maybe I sort of didn't really mention it at all."

"Mention what?" Mom asked.

"I'll just go start my homework too," I offered.

"Oh no, missy," Aunt Zephyr protested. "You're the whole reason I came here."

"Aleca?" Mom asked. "What does your visit have to do with Aleca?"

"So it's Aleca, then," Dad said. "I wouldn't have guessed it. I thought it was all over and done with."

"What's Aleca?" I demanded. "What's not over and done with?"

"Oh, enough with the pretending," Aunt Zephyr said. "One thing I'm not is immortal. I'm old, and when you're as old as I am, you don't have time to pussyfoot around. Now out with it."

She knew.

I don't know how I knew that she knew, but I knew. Aunt Zephyr knew, somehow, what I had been doing the past couple of days. But how could she?

"Alec," Mom said. "What's going on?"

"Let's all have a seat," Dad suggested. He nudged us over to the sofa. Aunt Zephyr took a seat in the recliner, where she removed her shoes and socks. She began wiggling her toes, which were crooked, but her toenails were painted the same shade of lavender that Dylan and her friends used. It seemed funny on such an old lady.

Dad cleared his throat. "Aunt Zephyr, maybe you should start with some background."

"Good idea, Skippy," Aunt Zephyr

replied. She looked at me, and her eyes twinkled. "Little miss, there's a lot about your family that you don't know . . . but you're about to find out. Hold on to your hat!"

✳ 12 ✳

My Grandfather, a Horse, and a Snake

Here is the story as Aunt Zephyr told it:

Once upon a time there were three babies. The Zamm triplets—my grandfather Alec; his brother, Zander; and their sister, Zephyr.

Life started out for the Zamm triplets normally enough. They lived on a farm, helped their parents with the animals, tended the garden, went to school, and played and fought like regular brothers and sisters—pretty much all the stuff you see in those movies about kids growing up on farms in the olden days.

It wasn't until the triplets turned ten that everything changed.

On the day of the triplets' tenth birthday, my grandfather Alec was out in the barn, brushing one of the horses. Suddenly the horse spooked. A bull snake had fallen from one of the rafters. The horse began bucking and kicking wildly. Alec was in trouble. He couldn't get around the horse to escape from the stall. If something didn't change fast, the powerful animal would kick him to death. Alec shouted at the horse, "Just be still! I'll get the snake!"

The horse replied, "Hurry up and get it, then! I'm scared of snakes!"

Yes. *The horse—as in those four-legged animals that are supposed to just neigh—replied, as in actually talked!*

But Alec didn't have time to stop and think about that. Instead he rushed to where the snake was hissing. He reached for a loose piece of wood in the stall and pulled it free. When Alec raised the wood to strike the snake, the snake began talking. "Take it easy! I just lost my balance! I didn't mean to scare anyone!" The horse stopped kicking. The snake stopped hissing. And Alec stood staring.

It was then that Alec realized the snake was talking to him and that the horse had just done the same.

"Well, what are you trying to do, get me killed?" Alec demanded.

"It was an accident, really," the snake said. "Look, you don't want to kill me, do you? I mean, look at the benefits of having me around. I'm better than any old cat when it comes to rodent control, am I right?"

Alec thought about this and had little choice but to agree with the snake. He looked at the horse. "He does have a point."

"I don't care if he does!" the horse said. "Snakes are creepy! Now get him out of my stall!"

"Consider me gone," the snake said. "I'll just ease through this crack right here, okay?" The snake slithered out where Alec had pulled away the piece of wood.

"Whew! Glad he's gone," said the horse. The horse and Alec stared at each other for a moment. Then the horse asked, "Why are you looking at me like that?"

"I didn't know horses could talk," Alec said.

"Don't be silly," the horse replied. "We talk all the time. In fact, we're quite chatty. I just didn't know that humans could understand us."

"Neither did I," said Alec.

"Well, what a relief, indeed," said the horse. "Would you mind running that brush along my left hip, please? I have a terrible itch. Ah, yes. Up a little more, if you please. Yes. That's the spot."

And so Alec spent the next hour in the stall, talking to the horse and wondering how in the world he was able to do it.

When he went inside, he was convinced he'd fallen asleep in the barn and dreamed the whole thing. It was too ridiculous.

But it was nothing compared to what had just happened to Zander.

❄ 13 ❄

Zander Zamm Makes a Deal

While Alec had been in the barn talking to the animals, Zander had gone to the little market up the road from the Zamm farm. His mother had sent him to sell eggs. Their chickens laid quite a lot of eggs every day, and the Zamms had an arrangement with Mr. Newman. Mr. Newman sold the eggs in his store, and the Zamms received a credit each week based on the number of eggs delivered. No money was ever exchanged.

The Zamms had thought Mr. Newman was kind to do them such a favor, as it helped them use the eggs to get what they needed.

On this particular day Zander presented two baskets full of eggs to Mr. Newman. Zander expected the usual credit for them. "I'm afraid that we're overstocked on eggs today and don't need two full baskets," Mr. Newman said.

Zander was worried. He needed a new pair of shoes for school, and the credit for the eggs would be helpful in getting them. "I'm sorry to hear that," Zander replied. Zander was in fact sorry. He was a straightforward young man who always said what he meant.

"I suppose I could help you folks out," Mr. Newman offered. "Tell you what I'll do. I'll give you half the usual price for the

75

second basket, just to take them off your hands. Better that you get half than nothing, even though I can't use them."

Zander was just thinking that this was a good bargain. Then he heard Mr. Newman say, "Dumb kid's going to fall for it. I'll make twice what I usually make on these eggs when I sell them."

It was strange, because Zander had heard Mr. Newman say it, but Mr. Newman's lips hadn't moved.

Zander stared at Mr. Newman, trying to understand what had happened.

"What's wrong with this kid? What's he staring at me like that for?" Mr. Newman's voice said. But again his lips didn't move. "So, do we have a bargain?" Mr. Newman said. This time his lips moved.

"You do need the eggs," Zander said. "You're not overstocked. You're trying to cheat us."

"How could you say such a thing?" Mr. Newman said, a shocked look on his face. Then Zander heard, "How did he know?" But Mr. Newman's lips didn't move.

"Serves him right, that old cheat." Zander turned to see Mrs. Hatfield weighing some dried beans near the cash register where Zander stood talking to Mr. Newman. Then Zander heard her say, "About time somebody stood up to that scoundrel Newman." Mrs. Hatfield's lips weren't moving either.

"So, what's it going to be?" Mr. Newman said with moving lips. "I hope he doesn't tell his father about this," he said without lips.

Zander realized he was hearing Mr. Newman's and Mrs. Hatfield's thoughts. That was why their lips weren't moving.

"Twice what you usually credit our account," Zander replied.

"Twice?" Newman gasped.

"Yes," Zander said. "Or I'll tell my father about this."

"Yikes. His father is big," thought Newman.

Zander said, "My father would be angry if he knew you'd tried to cheat us."

Mr. Newman smiled. "Now, Zander, would I do something like that?"

"Ha! You certainly would," thought Mrs. Hatfield. "You do it all the time."

"Twice as much for the eggs," Zander insisted, his face as hard as stone.

Mr. Newman swallowed with effort. He pretended to consult his ledger. "I've made a mistake. We're not overstocked on eggs. We're *under*stocked. Twice the value it is."

Mr. Newman signed the credit memo for Zander. "Say hello to your parents for me," he said as Zander turned to leave. Then Mr. Newman thought, "I hope he doesn't tell them about this."

"I will tell them hello from you," Zander said. "And that's all I'll tell them."

Zander kept his word. He never told his parents that Mr. Newman was crooked. And from that day on the Zamms got twice the price for their eggs at Newman's market.

✳ 14 ✳

Wondering

"Your brother Zander could read people's minds?" I asked Aunt Zephyr. "How?"

"Same way that my other brother, Alec, could talk to animals," she replied.

I repeated, "How?"

"Exactly," she said.

That did not answer my question.

"Alec, this doesn't make any sense," my mother said. "Is this a story to entertain Aleca, or is your aunt actually suggesting—"

"His aunt is sitting right here, Harmony," said Aunt Zephyr sharply. "You needn't talk as though I'm not in the room."

"I'm sorry," my mother said. She never liked to upset anyone. "I didn't mean—"

"No apologies necessary," interrupted Aunt Zephyr. "It is quite a bit to take in. But I believe it's best that we speak plainly. I've always been a believer in speaking plainly. Sit up straight, Skippy."

My father straightened his posture.

"I still don't understand how your brothers did such things," I said.

"Neither did we," said Aunt Zephyr. "We wondered about it for a long time— wondered how it had happened, wondered why it had happened, wondered how to make it stop happening, wondered why it had happened to us and not to other people."

"Us?" my mother asked. "You talk to animals and read minds too?"

"Heavens, no!" cried Aunt Zephyr. She laughed. "Imagine me, reading minds and talking to animals! How silly!"

My mom looked confused but laughed along with her. "Oh," my mother said. "For a minute there I thought that you were . . . you know . . . not ordinary."

Aunt Zephyr stopped laughing. "I assure you that I am far from ordinary. I didn't read minds or talk to animals, but I had my own reasons to wonder."

Then Aunt Zephyr told us what had happened to her on that same day so many years before.

✳ 15 ✳

Aunt Zephyr Wanders and Wonders

While her brothers, Alec and Zander, were having their own strange experiences, Aunt Zephyr was visiting her widowed aunt a few towns away. It was canning season, and young Zephyr was supposed to help Aunt Jessica put up pickles, jellies, and preserves. It was hot, tiring work—picking vegetables from the garden, slicing mounds of cucumbers, washing fruits, and boiling all those syrupy sweets all day with no air-conditioning, and sealing jar after jar of pickles. But the worst part was that, according to Aunt Jessica, Zephyr never did anything right. The spices were supposed to be in cheesecloth bags, not free-floating. The stove was too hot, and Aunt Jessica was certain the bottom of the pot would scorch. The jars hadn't been boiled long enough to sanitize them properly. Whatever the task was, according to Aunt Jessica, Zephyr did it wrong. "You're not worth your salt," Aunt Jessica told her. It was an old expression that meant you were useless.

That evening all Zephyr wanted to do was crawl under the covers and cry herself to sleep. But Aunt Jessica made her stay up and piece a quilt. Of course Zephyr did that wrong too. "Your stitches are too big!" Aunt Jessica railed. "Smaller! Smaller!"

Finally Zephyr had a thought. A very strong thought. The thought was, *I don't want to be here. I want to go home.*

Zephyr suddenly felt a strange sensation, something like a very forceful tug, but a quick one. So quick that she didn't have time to stop and think what this strange feeling even felt like.

The next thing Zephyr knew, she was home.

"Hi, Mama," Zephyr said. Her family was sitting in one room, reading together before bedtime.

"Zephyr!" her mother exclaimed. "How did you get here?"

"I don't know," Zephyr replied. "I thought a thought, and here I am."

"Aunt Jessica's house is near about

twenty-five miles away," said Zephyr's father. "Somebody drove you here in a car?" He looked out the window but saw only darkness.

"No, sir," Zephyr stated. "I thought a thought. That's all."

Zephyr explained to her parents over and over what had happened. They didn't believe her. It wasn't so much that they thought she was lying. They thought she was out of her mind. "Should we call the doctor?" her mother wailed.

But before that could happen, Alec spoke up. "I have something to tell you too," he said. He told his story about the horse and the snake to his astonished family.

"I have something to say also," offered Zander. Then he shared his story about what had happened at Newman's store. Except he left out the part about Mr. Newman being a cheat.

Mr. Zamm spoke up. "I have heard tell of strange things such as these before," he claimed. "My father died when I was young. But some say he could be in the same room with you and you'd never see him. His brother, my uncle, lived far away. I met him only once. But they said he could see and hear things that happened in the next county. I thought they were just good stories, something to whisper about for fun."

The Zamm family was up all night, wondering what these strange things could mean.

They were now inclined to believe that these abilities skipped a generation, like blue eyes or red hair. Maybe these powers were like the dimple in the chin that all three of the children had, like their Grandfather Zamm, but that their father had missed.

Yes, the Zamms had much to wonder about.

✳ 16 ✳

I'd Rather Be a Pretty Witch

I've never been very good at not saying what I think. So I went ahead and asked what I wanted to know. "Are we witches?" I said to Aunt Zephyr.

"What do you think a witch is?" she replied.

"Magic ladies who look like humans but aren't," I answered. "They live forever and ever and never get old." I had heard stories about ugly witches and pretty witches. Only the mean ones were ugly. I decided right then that I would be nice so that I would get to be one of the pretty ones.

"Young lady, you and I are not witches," Aunt Zephyr proclaimed. "Look at this." She pulled her face back to make her wrinkles go away, then let go so that they looked even deeper. Then she pulled up her sleeve and pulled the skin under her arms and knocked it so that it swayed back and forth like a hammock. "Deterioration is the way of all human flesh. As you can see, I am one hundred percent human."

I guess Aunt Zephyr wanted to be one of the pretty witches too. I was kind of disappointed.

"What do you mean by 'we'?" my mother asked. "Are you saying that Aleca talks to animals . . . or reads minds . . . or teleports?"

"Don't be ridiculous," Aunt Zephyr said, and chuckled. "Aleca can't do any of those things."

My mother breathed a sigh of relief.

"All she can do at this point is stop time," Aunt Zephyr continued.

"She can do *what*?" My mother turned green.

"Skippy, get the girl some smelling salts," Aunt Zephyr told my father. "I do believe she's about to pass out."

But my father was too busy staring at me. "Aleca can stop time?"

"How did you know?" I asked Aunt Zephyr.

"I was standing on the shores of Northern Ireland, watching the waves, when they stopped. Just as a wave was about to crash along the rocks, it stood at attention instead. That was my first clue. Then the next day I was in this lovely village in southern Iceland picking the most gorgeous purple flowers by a stream. Some birds flew by and then stopped and hung in the air like a mobile over a baby's crib."

"You mean time stopped all over the whole entire world?" I asked.

Aunt Zephyr laughed. "Silly child! Did you think you could stop time in one place only? It's an entire system—you can't just do it piecemeal. That would throw the whole thing out of whack." She said this like everybody should know it. I felt embarrassed for not figuring it out myself.

"But how did you know? Weren't you

stopped, just like everyone else?" I wondered.

"Child, if I were just like everyone else, I wouldn't be here right now, would I?"

"So you're saying that these . . . powers . . . abilities . . . ," my dad began, "don't affect other . . . witches?"

"Skippy," Aunt Zephyr said, snorting, "we are most certainly *not* witches. Weren't you listening?"

"If you're not witches," my mother said, "then what are you?"

"Harmony, Skippy," my aunt said, "fear not. Your daughter is *not* a witch." My mother breathed out a big breath. Then the gleam returned to Aunt Zephyr's eye and she announced, "Your daughter is a *Wonder*."

✳ 17 ✳

I'm Not a Dud . . .
I'm a Wonder!

"What's a Wonder?" I demanded. If I was one, I wanted to know what it meant.

"That's what my brothers and I learned to call ourselves," explained Aunt Zephyr. "We knew we weren't immortal, because our grandfather, who had been like us, had died, and so had his brother. We knew we weren't superheroes, because we didn't have super-strength and, more important, no one had given us a colorful costume. The things we could do didn't have any rhyme or reason that we could see. They were just strange abilities. We wondered what it all meant. My mother said that's what we were—Wonders. A 'wonder' is something that causes surprise, and we were certainly surprised."

"So am I," my mother blurted. "I'm so surprised, I think I may throw up."

"Aunt Zephyr," my father said gently, "how did you know that Aleca was the source of the time delay?"

"That's a story for another day," she replied. "I had a bit of information to go on, and yet . . . Wonders have a sense of things—a special sense that you Duds don't have. For example, if you heard a noise from the kitchen, how would you know to go and look in the kitchen instead of upstairs?"

"I guess I'd be able to hear where it was coming from," my dad answered.

"It's kind of like that," said Aunt Zephyr. "When time stopped, I could tell where the disturbance was coming from, so I thought a thought, and here I am. I came looking for the source. Other Wonders, you see, are immune to the, shall we say, *high jinks* of their peers."

"What does that mean?" I asked.

"It means that when you stop time, it doesn't affect me. Or anyone else of our kind. We go right on about our business as usual."

"Oh." I had so many questions; I didn't know which to ask first. "How'd you know it was me and not Dad or Dylan?"

"Well," began Aunt Zephyr, "it all made sense when I thought about it. I already suspected that the Wonder trait skips a generation, and since I was pretty sure your father was a Dud, I figured it had to be one of you children."

"Why didn't you think it was Dylan?" I asked.

Aunt Zephyr waved her hand and made a *pfft* noise. "You've heard the expression 'It takes one to know one'?"

"Yes," I replied.

"I could tell from a mile away that your sister was a Dud. She has 'Dud' written all over her. No offense, Harmony."

My mother shook her head and held up her hands. Her eyes were as big as fried eggs.

I guessed this was a lot for her, all in one day.

"You, on the other hand," Aunt Zephyr continued, "are a Wonder if I've ever seen one."

I sat up straighter without being told.

"Yes, you are obviously a Wonder," Aunt Zephyr went on. "And we are going to have to do something about that. Quickly."

❄ 18 ❄

There's a Downside to Everything

I didn't like the way Aunt Zephyr had said that something had to be done about my being a Wonder. I had just gotten the news that I was special, that I finally had a thing, and already someone was talking about taking it away.

Yes, stopping time had been kind of scary, especially because I didn't know how I had done it or why. But I wanted to find out. And once I found out, I thought maybe I might want to keep doing it. Now that I kind of knew what was going on, I could hardly wait to tell Maria.

"What do you mean we have to do something, Aunt Zephyr?" asked my mother. Oh good. She was asking for me so I didn't have to.

"Obviously," declared Aunt Zephyr, "we can't have a ten-year-old child in charge of the world's clock."

I guessed she had a point. Maybe when I was eleven? I asked that question out loud, but Aunt Zephyr shook her head.

"No one could ever be old enough to have that kind of power unchecked," she insisted.

Unchecked. So did that mean I could have it checked?

Aunt Zephyr seemed to have read my mind. I wondered if she had caught that ability from her brother Zander. "I can't take the power away from you, Aleca," she explained. "It would make things much easier for you and everyone else if I could."

"Easier?" I said. "Why would it be easier?"

"I know this is a lot for you to think about right now," my dad said. "It's a lot for all of us." He looked at my mother, then back at me. "But, Aleca, this is not fun and games. This is a very big deal. You need to listen carefully to what Aunt Zephyr is about to tell you."

Aunt Zephyr cleared her throat. "Do you know why you never met your grandfather?" she asked.

"Because he died before I was born."

"Yes. And do you know why?"

"No, ma'am."

"Because the man almost never got a breath of fresh air!" she exclaimed. "He had to avoid nature. You think it would be fun to talk to animals? Well, it wasn't. They never hush. They could tell by some instinct that Alec could communicate with them, and so they never left him alone. All the questions, concerns, and complaints they had about humankind, Alec got an earful. As soon as he was old enough, he left the farm and moved to the big city. Even there he carried an umbrella every single day, rain or shine, to hide from the birds. He avoided people with pets. Dogs on walks would drag their owners by the leash so they could get to Alec. 'I'm so excited! So many smells!' or 'Can I have a treat?' or 'I'm a good boy! I'm a good boy! I'm a good boy! Yes, I am!' And if he made the mistake of visiting someone with a house cat . . . Well, trust me. You do *not* want to know what cats have to say. In between demanding an explanation for laser pointers, they have a lot of criticisms about humans."

"So that's why my father would never let me get a pet," said my dad.

"That's not entirely true," said Aunt Zephyr. "You had a goldfish once. Alec told me about it."

"Oh yes." My dad nodded. "Strangest thing. It jumped out of its fishbowl and died. We found it lying there on the table."

"It was trying to get to your father," Aunt Zephyr explained. "It wanted to tell him a joke. Goldfish think they are funny, but they have no sense of humor whatsoever. Drove your father bonkers. Every time he walked past the bowl, it was 'Knock, knock' or 'Two halibuts and a clam are on an airplane' or 'Stop me if you've heard this one.' Your dad tried to avoid the table with the fishbowl, but the fish was so lonely, it forgot it couldn't breathe air and tried to go looking for your father. Goldfish! Terrible sense of humor and not very bright, either."

I had never thought about goldfish getting lonely. I suppose it must be boring, swimming back and forth all day long in those little bowls.

"And Zander—poor Zander!" moaned Aunt Zephyr.

"Poor?" I cried. "Couldn't he read minds? He knew everything!"

"Yes he did," agreed Aunt Zephyr. "And it was the most dreadful of burdens. Aleca, did your parents teach you how to be polite?"

"Of course," I said.

"What does it mean to be polite?" she prompted.

I had to think about it for a minute. "It means to not slurp your soup or burp and stuff. And to say 'please' and 'thank you' and 'how do you do?' And chew with your mouth closed. And to not say mean things." Then I thought of one more. "And to not say everything I think." Mom and Dad had to remind me about that one a lot.

"Exactly," noted Aunt Zephyr. "Polite people keep unkind thoughts to themselves. But for my brother Zander, there was no such thing as a polite person. He could read the thoughts of everyone he met. Every awful thing people thought, every sneaky motive they had, it was all laid bare for Zander to know. It was so awful, he had to become a hermit. He never left the house, ever. I used to come by and bring him food and soap. Especially the soap. And lots of it. Have you ever smelled a hermit?"

I shook my head because of course I had not smelled a hermit. But from the *ick* face Aunt Zephyr made, I guessed that hermits must be superstinkified.

Mom gasped. "Will Aleca have to become a hermit?"

"I don't want to be a stinky hermit!"

Aunt Zephyr, who had seemed lost in her memories, snapped back like a rubber band. "You won't," she assured me. "Not if

I can help it. Aleca, now you understand that you must learn to control your ability. Otherwise, your ability will control you!"

"Is that even possible?" my dad wondered. "Aunt Zephyr, can you control your ability?"

"Most of the time, yes," she replied. "It's been like my other, normal abilities, really. It took me years to grow into mastery. As a girl I had to be careful not to think too hard about any particular place, or the next thing I knew, there I was. But as a grown woman, for some years I was able to enjoy being a Wonder. In time I found my method of travel quite exhilarating, and indeed, I have seen the world. But as I've grown older, I find it has become more difficult. Just like my ability to run or to read without glasses has deteriorated, so has my ability to control my gift. But it takes extreme concentration. I cannot allow my mind to wander. Just last year, for example, I saw a postcard with a giraffe on it, and the next thing I knew, I was in Africa.

"Aleca," Aunt Zephyr continued. "I never had another Wonder to mentor me. That's why I'm here. I'm going to help you make the best of this."

I thought that sounded pretty good. "I still can't believe you knew it was me," I marveled. "From all the way in Iceland!"

Aunt Zephyr nodded. "Yes," she agreed. "And let's just hope I'm the only one who did."

❄ 19 ❄

Wondering Is Top Secret

"What do you mean, Aunt Zephyr?" my mother asked. "Who else would know about Aleca?"

"That's hard to say," Aunt Zephyr replied. "We have no way of knowing how many other Wonders are out there or who they are. Some may be good and some may be bad. I have suspected for some time that a Wonder—or Wonders—may have the ability to control the weather. It would explain the storms that come from nowhere and destroy without warning. Others may have abilities they use for good. Whenever you read a news story about a mysterious rescue, for example, there is always the possibility that a Wonder was involved in some way. Perhaps. Perhaps not. There is no way to be sure."

"Alec," my mother said. "That hailstorm the other day—it was eighty degrees outside, and then suddenly, hail the size of basketballs!"

"As I said," Aunt Zephyr continued, "we cannot jump to conclusions. We simply have to be open to the possibility. We also must consider that others who are not Wonders know we exist. They may be looking for us."

"I could be famous!" I said. I had always wanted to be on TV or get lots of hits on the Internet for doing something cool. I was already thinking about how charming and funny I would be when I went on the late-night talk shows.

"Absolutely not!" Aunt Zephyr said sternly. "You must never, ever tell anyone what you can do."

"Not even my best friend?" I protested.

"Not even your best friend," she said. "Even friends can't be trusted with something like this. They might tell someone else. They might be frightened of your ability. They might even stop being your friend."

I couldn't imagine Maria ever not being my friend. But then I thought about how Madison used to be my friend, so I supposed Aunt Zephyr had a point. Also, I thought again about how Maria had almost told me about my birthday present when I hadn't even asked for a hint. Maria could super-quick spill the beans on something like this without even meaning to. I couldn't tell her a secret this big and expect her to never let it slip.

"If there are people looking for Wonders," my dad said, "or other Wonders who are up to no good . . . what would they do if they found you and Aleca?"

"I have absolutely no idea," Aunt Zephyr replied. "And I don't intend to ever find out."

✳ 20 ✳

The One Time in History When Jolly Ranchers Didn't Bring Happiness

Aunt Zephyr had given me a lot to think about. Maybe that was why I couldn't sleep much that night. Or maybe it was because I had slept in that morning. Or maybe it was because Aunt Zephyr was sleeping in my room and she sounded like a gorilla with asthma when she snored.

But even being sleepy didn't prevent me from being excited to get my math test back.

The next morning at school, I could

hardly wait. In just a short time I would finally have that big red A and maybe even a smiley face at the top of my paper. I would finally get a Jolly Rancher, maybe even a red one.

What was weird, though, was that when I got the test back, I didn't feel excited anymore. I felt sad. Even though there was a big red A and a smiley face. Even though I got the Jolly Rancher. Even though the Jolly Rancher was red.

"Well, Aleca," Mrs. Floberg said, "I suppose you decided to study for once. You received the highest grade in the class."

Across the room at her desk cluster, Maria clapped. "Aleca! You did it!"

"Good job," cheered Joanie Buchanan.

"Way to go!" said Neal Martinez.

"High five," offered Scott Sharp, but I purposely missed his hand, what with all the nose picking I'd seen him doing lately.

"Thanks," I said to them all.

"Ooh, you got a red one!" noticed Joanie. "I got purple. Want to trade?"

Of course I did not want to trade a red for a purple, because it's not like I was born yesterday. "No, thanks," I said.

"Nobody trades red for purple, Joanie," said Neal. "You know that."

"Yeah, but I thought I'd ask just in case," said Joanie. "Somebody might like purple best."

Then I thought about how Joanie actually deserved her Jolly Rancher and how I'd cheated to get mine. "You can have my red," I told her. When she held out her purple one to trade, I said, "You can keep it. I don't really want one."

Joanie was excited. "Thanks!" she chirped.

At least somebody was happy, because I sure wasn't.

✳ 21 ✳

Something in the Lunchroom Is More Mysterious Than the Food

The rest of the day I felt rotten.

I had finally gotten a thing, and not just any old thing but a magical, supercool, amazingly awesome thing, and what had I done with it? I'd used it to become a big ol' cheater. On Monday I'd probably get the Civil War quiz back and feel rotten about that, too. I couldn't feel proud about good grades I didn't deserve.

Maria's excitement about my math test

grade made me feel even worse. "I'm so happy for you, Aleca!" she said at lunch. "*¡Qué bueno!* The highest grade in the whole class! You deserve it!"

I said thanks, but I couldn't really concentrate on the rest of what Maria said after that. All I could think about was how to undo what I'd done. But there was no way. I could stop time, not reverse it.

Since I couldn't go back and change what I'd done, I started thinking that maybe there was some other way to fix things. I remembered Mrs. Floberg showing us last week about how a negative number was the opposite of a positive number. If you added negative three to positive three, the result was zero. The one number canceled out its opposite. So I figured, maybe if I did a positive thing, it would work the same way and cancel out my negative thing. Then I'd be even. And it would be like the bad thing I'd done didn't count.

I tried to think of something good I could do by stopping time. If there was a bank robbery, I could stop time and disarm the bad guy and tie him up. Problem was, I didn't know when any bank robberies were going to happen.

Since stopping a bank robbery was probably out of the question, I thought maybe I could save somebody's life. Like, if I saw someone falling off a cliff, I could stop time and scoot them back so they wouldn't fall off. But there weren't any cliffs nearby, and we're not allowed to leave the lunchroom without a pass from a teacher, so that wouldn't work either.

While I was looking around the lunch-room trying to think of some kind of positive to balance out my negative, I noticed that one of the lunchroom ladies was carrying a steaming tray of hot dogs to the self-serve line. Just as she was about to go around to the front, her foot got caught behind a boy's foot, and she lurched forward. The hot tray, with a pan of almost-boiling water inside it, was about to fly straight out of her hands.

"Aleca Zamm!" I said. Everything went still.

This was perfect!

I got up from my seat and went to the lunchroom lady. I moved her foot away from the boy's foot and positioned it so that she'd be steady again. Then I moved her arms so that the tray was secure in her hands. I even pushed back into the tray the water that had already started to splash out. (The water that was in motion just before time stopped felt kind of squishy, like Jell-O. I could mold it any way I wanted until time started again.)

Now no one would get hurt. I'd done good deeds to erase the bad deeds. Keeping people from getting burned and also keeping hot dogs from being wasted were two good things, so I figured that would cancel out cheating on both of those tests. Okay, so maybe it didn't quite make up for cheating. Probably the only way to really make up for that would've been to confess to Mrs. Floberg. But I figured there was no reason to go overboard. I wouldn't cheat again, so the way I saw it, all I had left to do was not add anything bad to my list to mess up my good deeds–bad deeds math again.

There were temptations, but I resisted them. For example, I did not put chocolate pudding on the tip of Mrs. Floberg's nose. I did not even take a single french fry off anyone's plate, even though they smelled delish. And I did not even do anything gross to Madison's food. Of course, I can't take a whole lot of credit for that last one because Madison was not even there. She had checked out to go to the dentist. But maybe I would have left her alone anyway.

I was just looking around the room, taking in how still everyone was all at once, in what was usually the rowdiest place in the whole school, when I saw it.

It happened so fast, I almost thought I'd imagined it. But I hadn't. I'd seen it.

Movement.

Outside the school. Through the lunch-room windows, I'd seen a person's head darting away so I wouldn't see them. But I'd seen them, all right. I couldn't even say for sure what color their hair was, how tall they were, or even if it was a boy or a girl. All I knew was that someone was out there, unaffected by my stopping time. Just like Aunt Zephyr had been. Hadn't Aunt Zephyr specifically told me that other Wonders wouldn't be affected when I stopped time? So if somebody was moving around, that could mean only one thing.

I ran outside to see who it was, but there was no one there. I looked all over the school grounds.

Had Aunt Zephyr come to the school to keep an eye on me? No. It couldn't have been Aunt Zephyr. The person's hair definitely hadn't been the color of orange sherbet.

I thought of what Aunt Zephyr had said about other Wonders—some good, some not good. I thought about those people who weren't Wonders themselves but who were maybe looking for us . . . for reasons we didn't know.

I went back inside the lunchroom and sat down in my seat.

"Aleca Zamm!" I said.

Time started again, and I was glad—not only because the lunchroom lady didn't hurt herself or anyone else, but because the sooner time started, the sooner I could get home. And the sooner I could get home, the sooner I could tell Aunt Zephyr what had happened and figure out what it meant and what to do about it.

Yikes. She was going to be mad. She'd warned me not to stop time again.

The more I thought about it though, the less I worried.

How mad could Aunt Zephyr really be? After all, she was a Wonder, and nobody had made her stop doing her Wonder thing. She'd traveled all over the world, hadn't she? And she'd said that once she'd figured out how to use her ability, it had been "exhilarating." Yes, that was her exact word—"exhilarating." I remembered it because when she'd used it, I'd thought, *I hope I never get that word in a spelling bee.*

It seemed unfair that Aunt Zephyr got to be exhilarated by her Wonder thing and I didn't get to be exhilarated by mine.

I decided that when I got home from

school, Aunt Zephyr and I were going to have a serious talk.

I was going to figure out how to be a Wonder without getting caught. Aunt Zephyr could teach me. And when she did, there would be no stopping me.

Acknowledgments

Thank you, Abigail Samoun, for being such a fantastic agent and friend. This book happened because I felt comfortable enough to approach you about trying something completely different. Thanks for always hanging in and being so encouraging.

Thank you, Amy Cloud, for your amazing instincts as an editor. And for letting me be funny, or at least try to be.

Thank you to my family for your support. This is all so much more fun because I can share it with you. I appreciate all the feedback and great ideas from my children and my nieces and nephews. Dwight, thank you for always making sure I have time to write. I love you so.

Turn the page for a sneak peek at
Aleca's next time-stopping adventure:
Aleca Zamm Is Ahead of Her Time

What's Worse Than Getting in Trouble? Waiting to Get in Trouble!

"Where's Aunt Zephyr?" I asked my mom as soon as I hopped into the car after school.

"And hello to you, too," said my mom.

"Sorry," I said. "Hi, Mom. Where's Aunt Zephyr? Is she waiting for us at home?"

"I'm afraid not," my mother replied.

"Well, where is she?" I asked. "Will she be back soon?"

"I don't know," answered my mom. "I haven't seen her all day."

This was not good news. Because ever since lunch that day, all I'd been able to think about was talking to my weird, Wonder-ful aunt Zephyr. I hadn't been able to focus on anything else—not my school-work; not my best friend, Maria; not even my awesome birthday skating party happening the next day.

The reason I was thinking about Aunt Zephyr was because she was the only other person I knew who was a Wonder, like me. At least, that was what Aunt Zephyr called us—Wonders. The word referred to people who were able to do amazing, unusual things. Aunt Zephyr could think herself anywhere in the world she wanted to go. I could stop time—which, by the way, was something I was not supposed to do. Ever again.

But I had. That very day, in the school lunchroom.

I mean, I'd had a good reason and everything. At least I'd thought so.

Trouble was, I had kind of gotten caught.

Maybe.

Possibly?

Probably.

And so I needed to run this information by Aunt Zephyr immediately.

"I wish I knew when she was coming back," I said.

"Unfortunately, your aunt left without a word to anyone. I find that to be an *egregious* lack of good manners." I didn't know what that word meant, but Mom had dragged it out and emphasized it—"ee-GREEEE-gee-us"— so I figured it must mean something really bad if she took that long to say it. Then Mom added, "But what do I know? I'm just a Dud, after all."

My mom is usually very good-natured. In fact, her first name is Harmony, which is perfect because she has a talent for getting along with almost everybody all the time. But she seemed pretty annoyed about Aunt Zephyr's leaving without telling her. Plus, she hadn't been too thrilled when Aunt Zephyr had called her a Dud, which I guess might sound kind of harsh if you happen to be a Dud, but Aunt Zephyr doesn't mean it to be hurtful. That is just what she calls regular people who aren't Wonders like us. My sister and both of my parents are Duds, and so is everyone else I know except for Aunt Zephyr.

Oh, and apparently at least one other person.

I knew this because Duds are stopped along with everything else when I stop time, so they don't even know it's happening. I thought everyone at my school was a Dud, since everybody stops when I stop time. Well, I *thought* everybody stopped. But earlier today when I stopped time in the lunchroom, I saw someone's head move outside the window. It caught my eye, seeing as how it was the only motion there was. When time stops, trees stop blowing in the wind because the wind stops blowing. Stuff that was thrown up into the air stays there instead of falling back down. Birds and bugs stop flying and just float. A splash of water stands up stiff and stays there. Everything looks just like in a photograph. Nothing moves. Nothing makes a sound.

Except for other Wonders.

So when I saw the movement outside the lunchroom window, I ran to see who it was. But I didn't find anyone. All I could tell from the brief glimpse I'd had was that the person's hair hadn't been orange-sherbet-colored, so I knew it wasn't Aunt Zephyr.

Either another Wonder lived in our town, or someone had come looking for me. Aunt Zephyr had warned me that some Duds might be aware of us. That was one reason why I wasn't supposed to stop time, because there could be dangerous Duds lurking. Who knew?

So the person outside the lunchroom could've been a Dud who had figured out a way to become immune to Wonder-ing, or it could have been another Wonder who was not Aunt Zephyr. I had no idea how many other Wonders existed in the world, but it seemed unlikely that there would be another one in our little town of Prophet's Porch, Texas. I had to find out who it was and what they wanted.

But since Aunt Zephyr could think herself places in the blink of an eye, right then she could have been anywhere in the world.

I had to find Aunt Zephyr, fast, and ask her what to do about the person I'd seen outside the lunchroom window.

But how?

Sticky Situations
and Sneeze Stifling

When I got home, I looked all over the house. "Aunt Zephyr?" I called. I thought maybe she might be back from wherever she'd gone, but she didn't answer.

It was lucky for me that Dylan wasn't home from choir practice yet. She might have asked questions about why I was so worried about finding Aunt Zephyr. I didn't think Dylan was particularly fond of our aunt.

"Aleca, is something wrong?" my mom asked. "Did something else . . . happen?"

My mom and dad knew all about my being a Wonder. My mom had been pretty freaked out when she'd heard, because until then she hadn't known that Wonders even existed, and she'd certainly never met one. My dad hadn't been too surprised because he'd known that his dad and his uncle Zander and his aunt Zephyr were Wonders. Dad was a Dud because probably Wonderness skipped a generation or something. But at least he'd known what Wonders were. I guess that was why he hadn't had to take a headache pill and go lie down when he'd heard the news, the way Mom had.

"Aleca," Mom said now. "Is there something you're not telling me?"

I mumbled, "I kinda stopped time again today."

"You what?"

"I kinda stopped time again."

"Kinda?" my mom said. "Aleca, how does one 'kind of' stop time?"

She had a point.

"Okay, I stopped time," I admitted. "No 'kinda.'"

"Darling!" my mom said. She looked worried. "You know you're not supposed to do that anymore! It's dangerous!"

I felt bad, because my mom is awesome. Ever since I started kindergarten, she has put funny notes in my lunch box every day. She cuts my sandwiches into four triangles, just the way I like it. She doesn't get mad when I get a bad grade on a math test, as long as I try my hardest. She was letting me have my birthday party at the skating rink, with a cake from the fancy bakery downtown, and was even getting several of those shiny balloons that are four or five bucks a pop. (Not that you would pop them, but that is what people say—"a pop." Even about balloons.)

"I'm sorry, Mom," I said. "I was trying to help someone." I explained to her about how a lunchroom worker was about to drop a tray filled with steaming water. "I kept her from getting hurt. And I kept perfectly good hot dogs from going to waste. Two good things!"

Mom hugged me. "I understand, sweetie," she said. "But we don't know what bad things might happen if you continue using your . . . power."

"I know," I replied. I didn't have the heart

to tell her about the moving head I had seen outside the lunchroom window.

Just then the door opened. Mom and I both jumped to see who it was. But it was only Dylan.

"Choir practice got canceled." Dylan sighed. "Kelly's mom dropped me off. What's wrong with you two?"

"Wrong?" my mom asked. "Why would anything be wrong?"

"Because you both look like you just stuck your finger into an electrical socket." She meant that we looked jittery and crazy-eyed. And that is how you look after you stick your finger into an electrical socket. I know from experience. When I was little, I had trouble sometimes "making good choices" like they told us to do in preschool.

"Ha-ha-ha," my mom said. She didn't actually laugh; she said "ha-ha-ha." "Everything is fine. But you haven't seen your aunt Zephyr, have you? We've looked all over for her and don't know where she is."

"I haven't seen her," said Dylan. "You think she finally decided to leave?"

"She just got here yesterday," my mom answered.

"Long enough for me." Dylan scowled.

Mom didn't say anything.

"I've got homework," Dylan said, and went upstairs to her room.

It was only a few seconds later that we heard her scream.

Mom and I ran up the stairs to her room.

"What on earth?" Mom yelled. Aunt Zephyr was sitting on Dylan's bed, wearing only a towel around her body and a towel around her hair.

"I thought you said she wasn't here!" Dylan shouted. "Scared me to death, someone sitting on my bed when I opened the door! What's she even doing in my room?"

"A thousand pardons for invading your sanctuary," said Aunt Zephyr. "My aim isn't what it used to be."

"Aim?" asked Dylan. Then she whispered to Mom, "She is such a freak!"

"Dylan," Mom said. "You haven't had a snack since you got home from school. Why don't you run down to the kitchen and pour yourself a nice glass of milk? I made chocolate chip cookies."

"Cookies?" Dylan questioned, her eyebrows arched like rainbows. "All right. But can you please get her out of here?"

"Watch yourself, Dylan," Mom cautioned. "You will treat your aunt Zephyr with respect."

Dylan rolled her eyes but was too scared of Mom to say anything back. She knew she was one smart-mouthed comment away from losing her cell phone for a week, and as a middle schooler, Dylan did not think it was physically possible to live without her phone. She stomped downstairs.

Once Dylan was gone, Mom whispered, "Zephyr, we've been worried sick! Where have you been?"

"Finland," Aunt Zephyr replied.

"Why are you wearing towels?" I asked.

"I ran into an old friend," she said. "She invited me to take a sauna with her."

"What's a sauna, and where did you take it to?" I asked.

"A sauna, my dear, is a sweat bath."

"Gross!" I said. "I wouldn't take a bath in somebody's sweat for a million bucks!"

"The sweat is one's own," Aunt Zephyr explained. "It is produced by sitting in a hot room and relaxing."

"Wait. You mean you went all the way to Finland to sit around and get sweaty—on purpose—with a friend of yours?" I asked.

"Of course. In Finland it's very rude to refuse an invitation to sauna. What choice did I have? Besides, a nice, deep sweat is so invigorating. Do I look invigorated?"

"You look kind of sticky," I stated.

"If by 'sticky' you mean 'relaxed,' then you are correct," said Aunt Zephyr.

"You might have told me you were going to Finland," said my mom.

"I assure you, Harmony, it was a spur-of-the-moment decision. Spontaneity keeps life interesting."

"Well, if you're going to be spontaneous again anytime soon, could you at least leave a note?" My mom sighed. "Aleca has something to tell you."

"What is it, little miss?" asked Aunt Zephyr.

I gulped hard, like I was trying to swallow the news so it wouldn't come out. "I stopped time again today," I blurted.

Aunt Zephyr didn't look shocked. "Of course. I already knew that," she asserted. "Just as I was telling the most marvelous story, I noticed that Vilhelmiina failed to laugh at the best part, about the hippopotamus and the man in the trench coat. At first I thought Vilhelmiina had lost her sense of humor entirely. But then I realized that no one could *not* laugh at the hippopotamus-and-the-man-in-the-trench-coat story. So it stood to reason that either Vilhelmiina was dead or you'd stopped time again. I stepped out of the sauna and realized no one was moving, so I assumed the latter. But more to the point—did we or did we not discuss this just yesterday?" she asked flatly.

"We did," I said. "But see, I had this idea—"

"You had an idea," Aunt Zephyr interrupted. "So did the people who created cigarettes . . . or shoes for cats. Not all ideas are good ones."

I repeated the story about the lunch lady and how I'd wanted to help her. Then I tried to explain my theory that if I did a good thing when I stopped time, maybe it would cancel out any bad things I had done by stopping time before. When I said it out loud, my theory sounded pretty ridiculous.

"Wait . . . don't tell me," Aunt Zephyr said. "It didn't work out as you'd hoped."

"Not exactly," I said. Then I told her and Mom about the person moving outside the lunchroom window.

"Oh, Aleca!" Mom cried. "Who?"

"That's just it," I replied. "I don't know. I went outside to look, but the person was long gone."

Aunt Zephyr didn't say anything for a while. Her eyebrows were squished together so that the skin between them made a deep eleven.

"Aren't you going to say anything?" I asked.

"I don't exactly know what to say," declared Aunt Zephyr. "This is most troubling."